Dedicated to …

Kelly Lovell. Colleague. Friend. Soul Sister. Force of Nature. Game-Changer. Leader. Empath. Visionary. Fierce Flower-Wearer. Smallisall. Congrats on MyEffect and YOUNGA 2020.

Discovery Arts (www.discoveryarts.org) and Geek Club Books (www.geekclubbooks.com). The arts have the ability to change lives, families, communities and cultures. Marilyn and Jodi, you are tireless. You are fearless. You are crucial and appreciated.

To every non-profit and important cause that works so hard to be seen, heard and supported in order to make real, sustainable change in our world. To the initiatives and organizations with whom I have had the honor of working. The world is a better place -- and I am a better human being -- because of you.

Julie Dunlap. Editor. Bestie. Wit-extraordinaire. You are just a girl standing in front of a boy telling him to try it again (and again) until it is magic. Pai Gow!

"How to Save the World: Find a Smallisall" was written and published to support **YOUNGA 2020**; the first-of- its-kind virtual reality global youth takeover of the United Nations, Sept. 28-30, 2020. Young people and decision-makers co-create solutions for a better world. For more info, visit www.youngaforum.com. This is for YOUth.

D1021785

Also by Ron Roecker Available at Amazon Worldwide:

"They're calling him the next 'Mr. Rogers!' Ron Roecker's inspiring book series is exactly what we all need right now."
-Leeza Gibbons, Emmy-winner, NY Times Best-Selling Author

"6 OF 1/ HALF DOZ OF THE OTHER"
*Rhyming Book Series with DOs and AHAs
for the 5-Year-Old Kid to the Adult Who Once Was*

Book 1: Why Ball Wouldn't Bounce
"Best Children's Books of All-Time" and "Best New Children's Books to Read in 2020" lists by BookAuthority.org

Book 2: Why Inch Got a Foot
*4 out of 4 Stars: OnlineBookClub.org
5 out of 5 Stars: GoodReads, Amazon, Prairies Book Review*

"LIGHTLY SEASONED"
Seasonal Stories for Families & Friends

★★★★★★

"Knock, Knock! Trick or Treat!
A Fable-within-Fable of the Costume Enabled
with Gluttonous Fools and Ghastly Ghouls

★★★★★★

"Why Christmas is Cancelled:
Santa Spells it Out!"

available at

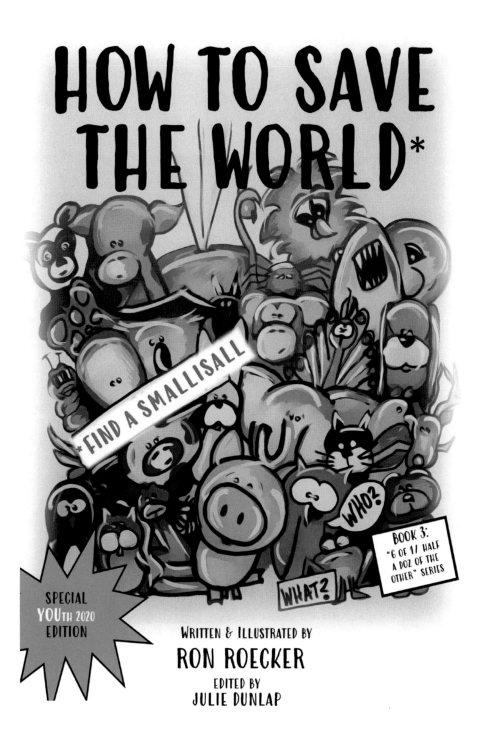

A day like today,
Starts off the same way,
No reason to think
twice about it.
You go 'bout your chores,
like each day before,
Then suddenly you hear
someone shout it:

"ATTENTION, I say!
They're coming our way!
The day we had hoped for is here!
We must be prepared
for their visits are rare.
No sightings of Smallisalls in years!"

The Smallisalls, Mama,
why all the drama?
said the busy, buzzing
bee to the Queen.
"Well, no one alive
has looked in their eyes.
'Til now, they have
seemed like a dream."

Then every flier
took wing to go higher,
As runners and swimmers
got movin'.
Spreading the news
to all points of view,
That Smallisalls soon
would be proven.

What's the big deal?
little pig squealed.
Who, Why & Whoooo??
asked baby owl.
What is at sssstake?
hissed the hatched snake.
Smalli-What? Who cares?
the cubs growled.

"We all should care,
my three baby bears.
And we have no more
time to delay.
The world has forces,
and we set courses.
And *tomorrow*
depends on *today*."

Then 'cross the land,
from ocean to sand,
The North Pole
to mountains and forests,
Young ones were told,
how history unfolds,
And how Smallisalls
might look before us:

The smallest of small,
they stand five coins tall,
Their long, pointy ears help them fly.
Their hearts beat in sync,
they know how we think.
Each Smallisall has 1-3 eyes.
Do not be alarmed,

but their legs and arms,
Can stretch 50 times from their middle.
They stand toe-to-toe
to make themselves glow.
They all love to sing and play fiddle.

When they all stand
--as one--
hand-in-hand,
The bond that is made
can't be broken.
Each one is quite strong,
and they all get along,
For only kind words
can be spoken.

And now for the myst'ry
of their part in hist'ry:
The Smallisalls' impact is treasured.
The good they have done
for E-V-E-R-Y-O-N-E!
Cannot be repaid, staged or measured.

"Like what?"

"What'd they do?"

"Come on, tell us,
PLEEEEASE?!"

They built a Great Wall,
Helped an eastern wall fall.
Smallisalls have superhuman powers.
They made Seven Wonders,
Saved koalas Down Under,
And lassoed that old leaning tower.

With Britain defeated,
A new flag was needed.
Betsy Ross had two stripes to go!
But she ran out of thread,
so the Smallisalls said,
"We'll be your string, Bets,
so let's sew!"

When people get sick,
The Hurt takes off quick,
So they had to make medicine fly.
They built a new plane,
that dropped meds like rain.
Then they said to the Hurt,
"Buh Bye,
Bye Now,
Bye Bye!"

When not from a sink,
most water sure stinks.
But Smallisall divers
are unsinkable.
They swim super-fast,
in a pond or a glass,
And suddenly
the water is drinkable.

You aim for the hole,
the ball stops to roll.
And you think,
"Oh, so close, yet so far!"
A Smallisall friend
might nudge it on in,
And SCORE!!!!
your life is on par.

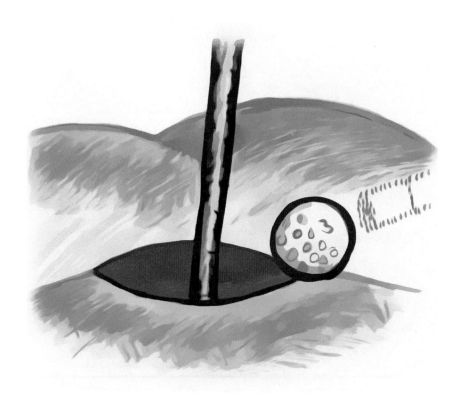

Sometimes your tummy
feels kinda funny,
But that is not
due to "butterflies."
The Smallisall tickles
when you're in a pickle,
Or when you are
excited inside.

Now that's just a list,
the historical gist,
Of big and small
Smallisall deeds.

"But why here and now?
And why us and how?
And what could
they possibly need?"

"No questions today,
they are on their way!
Why aren't all the ducks in one row?!!
We must be prepared,
with what must be shared,
Or they'll never come back,
so let's go!"

Then everyone jumped,
they all were so pumped.
With Smallisall tickles,
youngsters asked,

What can we *do to help all of you?*
(The tykes would take on any task.)

"Nothing, we fear,
You're too young this year.
There isn't a thing
you could do.
Except go and play,
Stay out of the way.
Once they get here,
someone will fetch you."

Then the ground began rumbling,
and things started tumbling!
As all the young creatures
stomped on earth!

Just like Smallisalls!
We're small, but that's not all!
We are giants
when it comes to our worth!

With thunder and lightning,
some a bit frightening,
The sky was turning black,
east to west.
Then all became still,
with a weird, silent chill.
And the old ones
looked down at the rest.

Then every creature
with its own features,
Regardless of species or size,
Started to wiggle,
a full-body jiggle,
then disappeared
before their eyes!

Poof!
There went monkey!
Pop!
Goodbye cow!
Poof! Pop!
The Inch worm and
Bird were gone now!

Poof!
Went the penguins!
Pop!
See ya spiders!
Poof! Pop!
Went blue whale and
the dolphin beside her.

Where they had stood,
they no longer stood.
They were gone in a flash,
just like that.
New faces confused,
New faces bemused,
They'd all been replaced
where they sat.

Every creature
now had the same features,
They all stood just
five… coins… high.
The same pointy ears…
and hearts without fear…
They could not believe
their new eye(s).

They weren't young or old,
no warm blood or cold,
No hunter or prey could be seen.
Some stood toe-to-toe
and, yep, they all glowed,
As they realized this was not a dream!

POP. POP. POOF!!!!!
(It's time for the truth!)

As fast as they turned,
adults now returned,
In what seemed like
a blink of an eye.
Every creature
again had its features.
And they all had one question:
"Why?"

As they were talking,
roaring and squawking,

They recalled
Smallisalls from their youth.

"We kids turned Smallisalls,
It was no dream at all!
They are a part of us,
that's the truth!

"The youngsters aren't here,
so it would appear,
They are learning
their power, as did we.
So let's take this time
to reset our minds,
and be the change
we all want to see."

POOF POOF POP POP!
(Will poof and popping ever stop?)

All over the globe,
cheers did explode,
As youngsters *popped*
back on their own.
Families were waiting
to start celebrating,
With hugs and global cheers
"Welcome Home!"

"What a huge day,
no day like today!
We can't wait
to hear about your trip.
You're now Smallisalls,
be proud and stand tall.
Of this iceberg,
you've just seen the tip."

The young looked around
and suddenly found:
That rhinos were talking to puppies;
Trees holding cats
who were hanging with bats;
And are seagulls
really laughing with guppies?

"What just occurred
is probably a blur.
Every question you have
must be asked.
The best thing to do
is share something new.
You could start with your
world-changing tasks."

After we changed
and grown-ups re-changed,
We were just a
little scared on our own.
We flocked together
fur, scales and feathers.
(When there are others,
you can't be alone.)
So, we took the chance
to give you a glance,
At how mighty and
strong we could be.
With Smallisall powers,
This would be the hour
to make our mark
on history.

All over the world,
unfed boys and girls,
And climate change
take a huge toll.
We focused on 'weather'
and 'hunger' together,
Problem-solving
was our main goal.

We stood hand-in-hand,
before they hit land,
Three hurricanes
had built strength at sea.
We flew to them first
and spun in reverse.
So Climate Change fallout?
Minus 3!

In a world of great haste
there is so much waste,
Yet so many have nothing to eat.
We tunneled through hills
and composted landfills,
So what's made and
what's needed can meet.

With global applause
from wings, fins and paws,
The youngest and smallest
all around,
Were now a strong group,
In Mother Nature's loop,
To Earth and to
each other were bound.

"It seems very clear,
that the species to fear,
Keeps harming our
land, sea and sky.
Humans alone
have endangered their own.
Earth isn't ruined,
although they have tried!"

United in rows,
they turned toe-to-toe,
Hands, paws, talons, fins
were held tight.

"We are tall-as-all,
'cause we're Smallisalls!
We have questions
for humans, please enlight:

Do you understand,
It is all in your hands
&
We're all getting
harder to find?

Why does the Earth
not hold enough worth?

Do you think you have earned
'Human-kind'*?*

They all looked around,
not making a sound,
For no one could speak
or tell lies.

And wouldn't you know,
They started to glow,
and lit up the Earth
and the skies.

Every generation
from every nation,
Must build on this
Smallisall tale.
If we don't step up,
our world will erupt.
And we all become
Earth's epic fail.

So when we reflect, asking,
"What's my effect?"
Don't say "that's too hard,
I'm too small."
For every good action
will cause a reaction,
In spring, summer,
winter and fall.

So, as this tale ends,
we know we are friends,
And that most things
can seem big and tall.
But pay that no matter,
'cause we can build ladders.
We "youth" must now
answer the call.

We all want to know,
before we must go,
Why did grown-ups
turn back to Smallisalls?

"Well, the older we get,
the more we forget,

There is
courage and power
in us all."

Yes, the world can be saved
Despite what's been paved.
There's an "I" and an
"All" in "Smallisall."

And today is our day,
for even giants
would say…

THE START

How to Save the World
A Smallisall 'Get Started' Guide
For Kids of All Ages and Sizes.

Activity #1: DRAW YOUR SMALLISALL
Based on the description given by the adult animals, come up with your own, unique Smallisall. Use a piece of paper or you can do it digitally, use different materials or whatever you want. Display your finished Smallisall where you and others can see it every day!

Activity #2: DISCOVER HELPFUL RESOURCES
United Nations 17 Goals to Transform the World.
From ending hunger and poverty and stopping global warming, to ensuring everyone has access to clean water, healthcare, education and employment, the United Nations has developed sustainable development goals and challenged every nation to be a part of the solutions. For more information, visit **https://sdgs.un.org/goals**

MyEffect: the mobile app and online platform connects youth and young adults to partners – brands, non-profits and influencers – and provides tangible steps for shared causes to create a true, measurable impact on the world. All actions and impact reporting are aligned with the United Nations' Sustainable Development Goals (SDGs). Visit **www.myeffectsolutions.com**.

Also visit **www.natgeokids.com** (search "Climate Change)

To get up-to-date info on Ron's books, fun facts and discounts, follow www.facebook.com/ronwroteit

Peace, Love, Truth, Kindness, Respect, Empathy, Unity, Action.

Made in the USA
Columbia, SC
23 October 2020